QUIET CREATURE
ON THE CORNER

QUIET CREATURE
ON THE CORNER

João Gilberto Noll
Translated by Adam Morris

Two Lines Press

O quieto animal da esquina
© 1991 by João Gilberto Noll
Translation © 2016 by Adam Morris

Two Lines Press
582 Market Street, Suite 700, San Francisco, CA 94104
www.twolinespress.com

ISBN 978-1-931883-51-1

Library of Congress Control Number: 2015958652

Cover design by Gabriele Wilson
Cover photo by Niall McDiarmid / Millenium Images, UK
Typeset by Sloane | Samuel

Printed in the United States of America

1 3 5 7 9 10 8 6 4 2

This book was published with the support of the Brazilian Ministry
of Culture / National Library Foundation (obra publicada com o
apoio do Ministério da Cultura do Brasil / Fundação Biblioteca Nacional) and by an award from the National Endowment for the Arts.

MINISTÉRIO DA CULTURA
Fundação BIBLIOTECA NACIONAL

ART WORKS.
arts.gov

A dark broth running from my hands beneath the faucet: I'd lost my job, and was saying so long to all that stubborn grease.

A dark broth running, there went three months, and I'd gotten into the habit of killing time by rambling through the center of town, a slight malaise if I saw myself in the mirror of a public bathroom, nothing a nineteen-year-old guy couldn't shake by sticking with it a little longer.

Sometimes, right up until I sidled into one of the job lines, I'd pull out any old piece of paper from my pocket along with a pen, and if someone saw me I'd put on a stern air, like I was taking note, not of some verses that sprang to mind, but of a reminder of some urgent obligation.

Through the center of Porto Alegre, without much variation, I'd stroll a bit through Rua da

Praia, have a coffee in the Galeria Chaves, hit the newspaper stand in the Praça da Alfândega, leafing, leafing, all the way up to Riachuelo, pop into a used bookstore, spend some more time leafing, poetry, too flat broke to buy even used books, money down near zero—and oftentimes, like now, I'd go sit in the public library up the street from the used bookstore, taking in the lives of poets, every one of them stranger than the last—there was one who was never looking to get laid, had never fucked anybody, died like that, chaste, and another who secretly collected his own fingernail clippings, he'd stick the clippings in a small jar and make a sort of relic of them, struck by some feeling he never knew how to decipher.

That afternoon it didn't take long for the same old hunger to hit me, so I went about getting up, leaving, gawking at the various people that were reading hunched over dark, coarse tables, the majority of them the same old regulars, and I got to imagining they were all unemployed like me, or that they collected a pension for some sort of hidden disability—I didn't see anything abnormal about them, seated there, reading, quiet, they didn't look handicapped, they weren't missing any obvious parts.

When I got to the door of the public library, soot was falling, and nobody could really say where it came from—in certain places so thick that you couldn't see the other side of the street. Some people went out anyway and got covered in soot, others ran, others were coming into the doorway of the library to take shelter. I took my wallet from my pocket and opened it, still had some cash, went out—the rain of soot was stopping—and went down Borges, took Rua da Praia to Vigário José Inácio, went into Carlos Gomes cinema, sat down to see a porno: the woman stopped the car with the top down and started rubbing her hand on her pussy, drawing a rowdy crowd of men around her, a Japanese tourist filming everything, and the woman like she didn't see a thing, eyes closed, cumming over and over, pussy slathered, pink.

It was almost late afternoon when I left the theater, and I went slowly, so slowly that I suddenly found myself stopped in Acelino de Carvalho alley, a chilly backstreet too narrow for direct sunlight, pedestrian-only, constantly reeking of piss, a couple barbershops on one side, three or four side-exit doors from the Vitória cinema on the other, hearing voices inside speaking English. Right then I remembered: I'm going home, and I walked resolutely in the direction of the bus terminal.

It was a Monday afternoon when I first broke into the apartment in Glória, where I've since lived with my mother. I went in alone, carrying just a box of tools, a box I used to carry, I'm not sure why, in tricky situations like that one. It was a halted construction project: a door here and there, some windows, bathrooms almost finished, kitchens less so. Every day new squatters discreetly turned up— my mother and I, in certain pauses, would look at each other, wondering, yet we decided to keep up the ruse by hanging things on the wall, pushing the broken china cabinet closer to the window. Ever since the eviction at that half-crooked house on the edge of the pavement right there in Glória, ever since then we'd been catching each other in locked stares, with a sort of stupor.

The bus that took me home passed along a ridge of cemeteries—I was surrounded by cemeteries on both sides, on this melancholy hill as they called it on the radio—every day from up there I saw the valley on the other side, the Glória neighborhood, full of low rooftops and the ugly church with towers that looked a little bit pink at that time of day.

I recalled my mother's face, waiting for me in the small apartment: just one room, brick walls exposed, bare lightbulb, and that woman who just seemed to wait for me—ever since my father took off, she was there without much to do except wait for me, waiting as she watched a black and white TV that didn't get all the channels.

Down below, the building had a big lobby full of columns, it was already dark when I arrived, and like every late afternoon, there they were, propped against the columns: a gang of kids, almost all of them out of work like me, a little pale under the weak lighting. I was in the habit of stopping to listen, throwing in my two cents if I could: a rumor that the military police might come in formation and throw us all out of our apartments by force, that it could happen at any moment—there was laughter from those who didn't want to keep talking about it, and then it was my turn to hold the slobbery joint. Two or three of them concealing syringes slunk off behind the building, where there were unformed blocks from a building whose construction was paralyzed almost right from the get-go, which we all called the ruins.

I opened the sagging door to the apartment and there was my mother, like always, waiting for me— only this time she was crying, saying she was leaving the next day, she couldn't live like this anymore, that I was young, but she was going to live with her sister somewhere on the outskirts of São Borja.

We sat down, leaned on the table. My mother remarked that the milk was thick. Indeed, there were rings of fat down the sides of the glass.

Someone knocked on the door, and I went to open it, already knowing who it was: the eldest son of the neighbor lady, a crazy kid who had this obsession with coming to ask me for a nail, and for the hundredth time I said I didn't have any more, but like always he needed to nail something—this time it was for nailing a beam, yes, nailing a beam in the ceiling above his mattress—he was almost shouting, and banging, banging, banging, until he bled. I looked up because that was the direction he was pointing so vehemently, I looked and saw the split ceilings in the hallway: I just need to borrow one nail, the kid was repeating, loan me one nail, that's all—the kid was gagging, and as usual he suddenly fell silent and returned to the apartment where he lived, with such a distressed expression that it seemed he'd just experienced a defeat that no other child was even capable of imagining.

While my mother was watching her soaps, seated on the shredded sofa, I went downstairs to see if anything was new, and I went down the stairs thinking of her: it really was a good idea for her to go to São Borja, because there was every reason to believe that everything was headed for collapse here in Porto Alegre, and then I wouldn't know what to do with her.

All around the building downstairs it was nearly a jungle, damp, parts of it always flooded, frogs croaking ceaselessly. There wasn't anyone there.

I leaned an arm against a column, stared down at the floor, my busted sneaker. I could take advantage of the silence to write a poem, pull a piece of paper and pen from my pocket: images of undulating things pursuing me, perhaps a thin stem, very thin, adrift on the breeze. That was when I heard someone singing, a high-pitched voice. I looked around—undulating things, the thin stem, very thin, adrift on the breeze would have to wait for another time. I went looking for the person who was singing—it had to be nearby, it wasn't coming from upstairs in any of the apartments—my steps drifting, looking in all the corners, the voice quite high, I went toward the ruins behind the building, where the voice seemed to be coming from, ah, it was the girl that lived on the top floor, Mariana if I'm not mistaken, seated on a chunk of ruin, younger than me, singing a romantic ballad by a singer who was hideous but provoked hysteric screams from girls in auditoriums on TV—hey, I said to her, you all alone out here?

The girl kept singing a while longer, then suddenly stopped and said, with the sky the way it was tonight, so full of stars, with the moon so high, it was likely the Druidesses would be descending in droves. This girl was like that, always talking about Druidesses and other strange beings—she said she never went to school, that she went every day to her hideout on the top of a hill, and stayed there singing all morning long.

When she started up with the thing about Druidesses my first reaction was to think of how sleepy I was, that I'd go to bed, or maybe get back to that poem.

But a second later, when she began to sing once more, I saw that, no, it wouldn't be so bad to hang out a while longer, it wasn't cold, so I stayed, wandering through the ruins, and she started singing a song that wasn't half bad. The night was clear and the ruins were yellowed by the moon.

Suddenly I realized I was so close to the singing girl that I could almost feel her breath—I didn't say anything, she stopped singing, I noticed there was a speckled wall that hid us from the building—I hit her with a kiss, and she fell with me onto the wet earth, my tongue passing through a murmur stifled in the girl's mouth, for sure a scream if I were to take my mouth off hers, and it was too late, I needed to suffocate that scream—I came right as my dick went in, and that dry murmur, the shout I suffocated by crushing my mouth against hers stopped—and I got up.

I went back to the apartment. My mother was sleeping on the shredded sofa with the light on. I went to my room, threw myself on the bed, and fell asleep.

I awoke in the middle of the night to voices outside, got up, went to the corner of the window, and saw the military police talking to some guys that were getting out of a red Escort, and a station wagon with a spinning light on top. The wagon had parked diagonally in front of the Escort, one of them started cuffing the guys, the other pointing his gun.

It was routine to be awakened during the night by troubles like these in the neighborhood: police, car thieves, drug traffickers, even on a calm night like this, it wasn't strange for shots to ring out, and there I was, like on so many other late nights, peering from the corner of the window, not wanting to be seen, because if I were I'd certainly fall under some kind of suspicion.

I sat down on the bed, listening to the police siren. Then the silence returned. In the living room my mother was snoring, tomorrow she'd go to São Borja.

I saw a bolt of lightning cut the sky, everything went blue, then came the thunder. I returned to the window and another lightning bolt illuminating the sort-of clearing where they were constructing the building next door: the Escort was still there. I doubted I'd be able to sleep with a downpour starting to rail against the window, the water blocking my view outside. I thought how my life was really taking its time figuring things out, and my mother snored as if saying don't even start—and there I was, staring at streams of raindrops that wouldn't let me see outside, unable to sleep, without even a way to take a walk in the street due to the rain, so I went to the living room, the light was still on, and I could've stolen my mother's wedding ring right off her finger, and even taken my time rolling out since she wouldn't wake up, but that wedding ring probably wasn't worth a nickel, and I was a coward anyway: I called out to her, asked her to make me a tea because I was feeling woozy, ready to vomit.

Early the next morning I took her to the bus station, she was leaving at eight, the rain had stopped, but the sky hadn't opened up, clouds were moving along lashed by a wind that seemed to come from the south, the temperature had fallen, my mother kissed me, I said that she was doing the right thing by moving to another city, and the bus left.

I went up Borges and jumped on the bus back home, and right when it was passing along the ridge of cemeteries, I looked down again at Glória, the church towers, coughed, spat out the window, crossed myself furtively, laughing to myself, pulled the cord for a stop, got off, said hello to a neighbor with a kid on his lap, took a shortcut that led over to my building, I was already in the clearing around the building and could smell the eucalyptus, I saw a paddy wagon and two military police talking with a guy who saw me and said: that's the guy.

There were five prisoners in the cell they stuffed me into. I've never seen people as ruined as those five, there were scars and sometimes holes all over their entire bodies, mouths completely toothless, one of them with a harelip that had never been sewn, but even worse than the toothless guy was the one with a single rotting, snaggletoothed canine, bleeding.

But before that I had waited hours for the sheriff—the police searched me all over, took a wad of papers with my poems on them from my pocket, spread the papers over the sheriff's desk, and when he arrived they started asking me if I had brothers, a mother or a father still living, and when I told them how my father took off and my mother and I had fallen into poverty, that I had to leave school to eke out a living for us both, the sheriff seemed to take a real interest: he leaned in close, thumped me on the shoulder, and yelled for me to tell him all about that time, that was the reason for everything, that was where it all had started.

Go ahead, he finished, impatiently.

So then I told him about those days, an assortment of things from here, leaving things out there, and when I got to the previous night, his eyes bulged at me, another thump to the shoulder when I said I'd stayed at home, that I'd gone to bed early, early

JOÃO GILBERTO NOLL

because I had to take my mother to the bus station.
He called over a police reporter, a completely blond
man—the tufts of hair coming out of his ears, even
those were super blond.

"Let's hear it," the reporter said, gathering up
the papers with my poems.

Then came the jailer to take me to the lockup.
When I got there one of the prisoners asked me
what time it was, another if I had anything to give
him; another said he'd strangle me at night, another
that he knew I was a poet, and that I should write a
poem in charcoal beside his mattress. The fifth one
didn't say anything.

That night the five of them made a big racket
masturbating, the bunks squeaking, the guys slap-
ping the walls, their labored breathing audible when
they came, nearly bursting. I was the only one lying
on a mattress directly on the slab floor. Waiting out
the sleepless night, I knew that if I stayed there
much longer I'd end up taking part in the communal
jackoff session.

Then they were snoring and it was dark, the only
light a single bulb that was swaying in the drafty

16

corridor. The window in that little hole had iron bars that left such a narrow space between them that not even an arm would fit through—I took a stool from under one of the beds, pushed it against the wall, got on top of it, and peered out at the night through the bars. A guard was passing hurriedly in the distance in front of me, a rooster began to crow.

While I waited for daylight I'd stay put, seeing if maybe some verse might emerge—maybe I'd have to get used to this, get close to these guys, figure out a way to escape. Or maybe it wouldn't be so rough—I'd at least have some company with those five guys, if I stayed with them through what would come, with those five spent and stinking bodies, so I'd need to see them without repugnance, be able to put an arm around them, talk to them, hatch a plan or something with those ugly, spent men.

When it gets light out I'll turn to the interior of the cell, and the newspaper with the story about me will be passing from hand to hand, and this will calm me, restore my sleep, because the five will see proof that I am one of them.

The day was breaking as I walked around the

cell, and for every eye that opened, every stretch, yawn, fart, belch, I was there watching, and I did the same myself, stretched, yawned, pretended to fart, belched, and this was how I managed to penetrate that set of ugly, spent bandits.

A prison bitch with a turban on her head appeared on the other side of the bars and passed a newspaper to one of the prisoners: the paper was already open to the police blotter, and there was my photo—me seated there in front of the sheriff, my busted sneaker—and beside my photo a three-by-four-inch portrait of Mariana.

I didn't get to read anything written in the story, not even the headline, I only had time to see the photos—I wanted to take advantage of the bitch's presence somehow, so I could, I don't know, say I needed to talk with the sheriff, so maybe she could do me a favor and talk to him. Sure, the bitch replied, smiling—she couldn't stop smiling.

Do me a favor, I repeated, and the urge to shake the bars came over me—I went as far as clenching the bars, but as I was about to shake them the urge to vomit overtook me and I stopped.

I saw that the bitch had taken off. My cellmates were making a big commotion with the newspaper, calling me a retard and letting out the strangest cackles—the way I'd like to laugh if I were so bold.

In that cell retard became my name. I went closer and mentioned taking the newspaper from them. They held me down and started tickling me, poking me, yanking on my dick—one had huge fingernails, he could only scrape when he touched me. In the middle of the confusion someone bit my hand, CHARGE! I yelled, and I threw myself headlong into one of their black leather jackets, I headbutted two, three times against the jacket of I couldn't tell which prisoner, my head spun, and then my eyes hurt. I felt like I was on the verge of the flu.

I was wiping snot on the sleeve of my shirt when I heard a voice from behind me calling: the jailor, telling me to come with him.

The metal bars half opened and I went out, the jailor steering me by the arm down the corridor, I heard the murmur of the sheriff's room, but when I got to the door they all fell silent, two flashes exploded, I noticed a huddle of reporters in a corner taking notes, and then suddenly the huddle broke open and they too went quiet, and in the middle of the reporters Mariana's scared expression appeared: she looked panicked, regretting that she'd reported me to the police, and from the looks of it she would have asked me for help if she could—she was so young and was so flagrantly scared, there, in the middle of those reporters asking her questions—I went toward her, but when I got close various arms detained me. Mariana took three steps in my direction, slightly lifted her arm as if to reach out to me, maybe to undo her denunciation, but she knew it was already too late.

They pulled her away and took her through a door beside the sheriff's desk. Strangely, I didn't see the sheriff. I felt a touch on my shoulder, looked back, it was a man wearing a hat and a black overcoat—he reminded me of a photo I'd seen of a street in Vienna in the thirties—and he didn't take his hand off my shoulder, just told me I was coming with him, I was leaving this place, I was going to a clinic in São Leopoldo, and he handed me a package, telling me that inside were some books of poetry and some paper for me to write on.

Wow, I sighed to myself, my entire life looks like it's about to change. More flashes exploded, and I said that yeah, I was ready, we could go.

The reporters and photographers stopped at the door to the sheriff's office, the man opened the car door, I got in, and he said, softly: and now São Leopoldo.

The clinic was a two-story building: we walked in through a garden full of arbors, with a white statue of a reclining woman pouring water from an amphora resting in her hands—the amphora was the source of a stream that ran beneath a little bridge we were crossing. On a plaque over the door was written ALMANOVA CLINIC.

I looked at the man, he seemed imperturbable, like someone whose sole mission was to install me in that clinic. We went up the steps, walked down a long hallway, he stopped in front of a door, opened it, asked me to enter.

I sat on the first thing I saw, a bed. A bed with a white sheet, a flattened pillow. The man asked me to lie down. I thought it was a good idea to try to sleep at last.

I dreamed I was writing a poem in which two horses were whinnying. When I woke up, there they were, still whinnying, only this time outside the poem, a few steps away, and I could mount them if I wanted.

I gave a few good pats to their haunches, and guided them, with waving movements of my out-stretched arms, into a fenced pasture.

About a hundred yards away, on the top of a low hill, was a wooden house, yellow, puffing smoke from the chimney.

I went into the house and saw Mariana. She doesn't have teenage breasts anymore, I muttered to myself.

We sat down to have some coffee, on opposite sides of the table. Mariana spread grape jelly on some bread, then handed me the slice.

I touched Mariana's leg under the table. She trembled softly. I kneeled on the floor, crawled under the table on all fours, and started to lick her thighs.

The bedroom was dark, beside the bed a lit candle. On the wall, shadows. The wind was blowing outside. Mariana was lying down admiring the shadows—I got on top of her, calmly, very calmly, as if some unknown plan were guiding my instincts.

I woke up at the crack of dawn to get some milk from the corral, now that I was doing the milking in the mornings.

As I made my way to the corral with a pail in my hand, the sun was starting to rise: roosters were crowing, birds flocking. I went along a path through fields of low crops.

When I got to the corral, it was still a bit shadowy, but it didn't take long to brighten up. Before sitting down on a stool next to the cow, I liked to make a few preparations for my daily chores—obsessively inspect the hay, make sure everything was tidy—I needed to straighten up in the morning, remind myself that Mariana and I liked to fuck in the hay. The first few times we got up feeling all itchy, but later we got used to it, to the point where one day we realized we no longer remembered to scratch.

After returning with the full pail it was already what you might call morning: the rooster had already shut up, and if the birds were still singing it wasn't really noticeable.

I remember the morning when, returning from the corral, still in the middle of the path, I heard my son crying from afar for the first time. He's getting to be strong, a real man, I thought. I opened the door—Mariana was breastfeeding the boy.

One night in bed, I brought my hand to rest in the wetness between Mariana's legs, and said I wanted another son. It was a cold night.

It was freezing when I woke up, and I grabbed the pail and went out across the gravel with my coat collar turned up, thinking that now that it was winter the nights would be getting longer, and when I got to the corral I'd have to wait for a while before it got bright enough to do the milking.

I opened the gate, there was some light in the corral, I looked back and saw it was the moon, dim as it was, that dimly lit the spaces between animals. The cows started to moo. I walked toward the back of the corral, to the haystack.

I stopped, a few steps away from me was a dark shape.

I had a flashlight in my pocket, I shone it on the dark features: it was the man who had picked me up from the sheriff's and brought me to Almanova Clinic. Even though I hadn't thought about that slice of my life in a long time, the memory of this man occurred to me naturally, without any effort.

There I was, with the flashlight shining right in his face, but I forgot to say something, and by the looks of it he had, too.

"You need to go back," the man said finally.

"And Mariana? And my son?" I asked.

The man came closer, shook me lightly, telling me the day to leave the clinic had come, and now I'd be going back home.

I took a few steps back, recoiling—I didn't want to return.

The man came and touched me on the face, and made me look around a room with gray walls that it took me a moment to recognize.

He was beside my bed, wearing a dark suit, hatless: he had very white hair, seemed much older than before.

He showed me some new clothes folded on a chair. The wool shirt was too big, the velvet pants fit like a glove, the shoes too—I remembered my busted old sneaker, at the moment the only thing from my past that would come to the surface—and I felt forgotten, foolish, dumbstruck.

I didn't see a mirror in the room, I pushed a button, they opened the door, I asked for a mirror. The only mirror was in the bathroom, shared by everyone on that floor. In the bathroom there was a man in a white smock, seated, discreetly watching how close the patients got to the mirror.

I had long hair, a full beard—I'd never let it grow before. Some time had passed, I could now see, and not a little: those long hairs and that thick beard were signs of its passing.

When I returned to the room it was empty. On the dresser were some books, all of them hardcover—I took one with a red cover, opened it: on one side poems in German, the other side translated to Portuguese. Various poets…Hölderlin—the name was pleasing to me.

Then I picked up some of the loose-leaf paper from under the stack of books, on them were poems written in my hand, all with my signature, a bit shaky, but I could tell it was my writing, they weren't forgeries.

I liked one of them as soon as it caught my eye; it spoke of some lucid drops.

The man opened the door, now dressed like he was the first day I saw him—black overcoat and hat. He said that I'd be accompanying him to a religious ceremony right there in the clinic.

We went into the room for religious functions, people were standing around talking in groups, it seemed more like a party. There were no chairs, the walls were smooth, nothing that recalled an altar. I didn't understand what was about to happen, everybody was speaking German.

I heard them call the man Kurt. Sometimes Kurt would turn to me and say something in Portuguese. He told me that these were all the latecomers. Yes, *latecomers*, I heard the words distinctly. And that they were getting together for a very special moment. With every new piece of information I nodded my head, trying to demonstrate respectful interest.

When I was about to ask what this moment would be, they tugged Kurt by the arm and everyone began to sing. By the sound of it, a German religious hymn.

The pastor, dressed in something that looked like a nightgown, black, over his suit, was in front of everybody else—young, very blond—except he wasn't singing, he seemed to be awaiting the end of the hymn so he could speak.

Obviously, the pastor's speech was in German. At the beginning it gave me the impression of a mild homily. However, he slowly elevated his voice until he reached a hard vehemence.

I whispered in Kurt's ear that I had a headache, I was going out to the garden to see if that would help.

I walked down a narrow path, listening to my steps on the flagstones.

Inside they'd started singing in German again.

I'd arrived at the gate to the clinic, slightly ajar. I didn't see anybody guarding the entrance.

Why not escape? No...it didn't seem like by going it alone I'd be able to facilitate the unfolding of things.

I asked a guy who was passing on the sidewalk for a cigarette. I took two drags and threw the cigarette on the ground. The German hymn was going

QUIET CREATURE ON THE CORNER

strong. The guy who'd given me the cigarette turned around and looked at me like he was wondering what my deal was.

What's up? I muttered, and turned back down the path. Everything was very quiet, the singing had stopped, as I got closer to the clinic building, I began to hear the pastor's speech once more, this time less exalted.

Suddenly I was very dizzy. I steadied myself on a tree, managed to estimate the distance between myself and the building, and decided to sit on a bench in the garden instead.

The murmur of water coming from the amphora… The participants in the ceremony began to say a collective prayer. O Father—it came to me involuntarily, like a poem—O Father, when will I be with you, at last? I looked at my new shoe stepping onto the wet earth—it made me want to laugh. I swallowed the laugh, but the mere thought of laughter caused the vertigo to recede. I remained seated there a while longer, breathing deeply, staring at my new black shoes.

Kurt was now driving his car, I at his side, on

the tape deck a German chorale—Bach, as I read on the tape case—Kurt seemed to follow along, moving his lips almost imperceptibly. At the moment the car was passing through the streets of Porto Alegre, finding its way out of the city—for a while a highway with half-potholed asphalt, countryside all around, few trees, until we turned onto a dirt road with more vegetation. It wasn't long before a large estate appeared at the end of the road.

"Where are we?" I asked.

"It's our house," as he was parking the car.

On the porch was a man, a relative a few years younger than Kurt.

This is the boy, Kurt said to the man, and then he introduced me to him—Kurt said rapidly: Otávio.

We went down a hallway, Kurt opened a door.

"This is your room."

The room was spacious, the walls nude, I thought later about filling them up with posters, and the image came to me: a man in black and white with a dangerous scar on his temple, his face enraged, covered in sweat.

I saw a desk, knocked on the wood to make sure it was real, thought that here I'd write my poems… maybe it would be nice to move the desk closer to the window, so I could write while looking outside. Out front was a row of eucalyptus trees.

I opened the drawer, there were blank sheets, I sat down.

I began writing a letter to my mother. The first idea that crossed my mind when I picked up the paper was that I wouldn't let her know where I was. If this house where I was staying was offering me, as they say, a new home, then fine, I'd stick with it as long as they didn't give me a hard time, and I was sending a letter only to inform her that I was doing fine and that she wouldn't hear from me any time soon, since the time I had would now be devoted to writing my poems, and writing letters would rob me of my time for poetry, and I was doing well, much, much better than she could ever have imagined.

In another drawer there were envelopes, and as I folded the letter and stuffed it in an envelope I felt the pleasure that I usually felt when I told a fat lie, the feeling of completely pulling the wool over somebody's eyes—a thing I knew how to do in writing but not speaking—into which would creep the compulsion to be caught lying: I guess I'd get a cunning glint in my eye, look askance, I guess my face burned with a fire I could extinguish if I really wanted to, but this time, since I was writing someone a lie that I had the feeling they were ready to believe, I got swept up in euphoria, as if I were close, very close, to a state that would represent for me, just maybe, a kind of emancipation.

At the lunch table there were three people besides me: Kurt at one end, Otávio at the other, and a woman with blue-rinsed white hair across from me. Kurt introduced me: Gerda, his wife, silent most of the time. She asked me my age then drank a sip of white wine from her glass.

Kurt had the same solemn air as his wife, Otávio did not. Otávio seemed like the plebeian of the household, besides the maid, obviously, who served lunch and stared at me curiously, lowering her eyes theatrically when they encountered mine.

Otávio was the one spinning the yarn, even though at times he obeyed the long silences I'd say were almost tense, if it wasn't for the sound of dishes and silverware slightly diluting the exposition of those pauses.

I'd never eaten so well and was hoping the wine would be at all future lunches. Everything led me to believe that my time had arrived, and I'd cling tooth and nail to this unique opportunity that had come out of nowhere and was heading who-knows-where—that's right, I'd never let it escape, even if I had to do exactly what they wanted, this was mine, and the best thing would be for me to forget my shitty past.

Seated at the desk in my room each day I tried to fill the blank pages in the drawer, writing my lines as I looked out the window at the eucalyptus, and as I wrote, the image of the eucalyptus overflowed and occupied my entire field of vision until it became something I could no longer distinguish, until I suddenly returned to the things that surrounded me inside that big house: those two men, Kurt and Otávio, and that woman, Gerda, who all seemed to want me there, without even asking for anything in exchange, as if they only wanted my negligent company as I wrote my verses, a silent shepherd guiding them to old age.

A fog. I put my hands in my pockets and went out for a walk—a few swallows were eating the still-warm shit of a horse that was wandering away through the pasture—I saw a gymnastic bar, ran, did a few somersaults around the bar, hung by my arms, did some chin-ups, broke a sweat, swayed with my arms stretched out, finally jumped off, slipped, fell, clapped one hand against the other, got up, ran, went up a small hill, saw that on the other side two men were fighting at the foot of the hill, and those two men were Kurt and Otávio. Even in the fog I could tell they were wounded here and there, blood at the corner of Kurt's mouth, on his shoulder, and down Otávio's arm ran a thread that, from that distance thick with mist, looked more black than red. They were fighting in silence, sometimes falling and rolling together, hurting themselves even more.

Suddenly they ceased fighting, stopped in front of one another, half staggering, then went their separate ways. From his shaky gait, Kurt looked to be the more afflicted.

Kurt didn't turn up at dinner that night, Gerda said he had the flu, Otávio was eating more than usual, talking with Gerda about the number of days that remained before he commemorated his return to Brazil from Italy as a grunt in the Brazilian Expeditionary Force.

On my evening walks I usually avoided the shed where Amália, the maid, slept, at the edge of a black and muddy lake, but that night when I realized I was standing in front of the boards that formed the door of the shed, I got the urge to knock—Amália opened, asked if I wanted to come in, a little cold inside, in the roof of the shed were open slats, the half-moon.

I sat on the bed, there was only the light of a candle on the nightstand, a radio I couldn't see was playing some Paraguayan folk music, a harp, a man singing in Spanish of grinding rocks between his teeth, such was his passion for his absent love—in the darkness, smelling the heavy scent of the sheets I felt like playing dead or pretending I was a fag or something. I'd let Amália take all the initiative, even if I were on the edge of cumming I wouldn't move a finger in her direction.

Amália lifted up a corner of the mattress,

brought out some newspaper clippings and showed them to me: it was the news from when they threw me in jail, but I didn't look long enough to see, averting my eyes as if none of that had anything to do with me. Amália brought the candle closer, looked at the photos, then watched me look away, confessed that she found me different, very different, she didn't know just how, she was kneeling on the floor between my legs, asking if she could sit beside me, but I didn't say anything, closed my eyes, and with closed eyes I saw a tremble in the shadows provoked by the flame. I let Amália's mouth kiss across my chest, nothing in me reacted, just intensified breathing, the sound of my zipper, the wet mouth, hot, descending, but I was quiet, not moving, Amália was sitting on my legs, she was getting there, now she was licking my closed eyelids, calling me lover, lover came out of my mouth without my meaning it to, lover, I repeated and I came—and I opened my eyes.

From then on we met every night in the shed. On the first night it felt like springtime, as soon as I got there Amália leaned up against me, put her arms around my neck, and whispered that she knew I wanted a son. She told me she'd read in a report that I confessed the desire for a child moments before entering my cell, and on that occasion Amália wanted to write me a letter, so that if she'd known how to find the right words, she'd write to offer to be the mother of my child.

Amália told me more, that one drunken night I'd babbled in my sleep about the story of a child who woke up crying as I went through the dark on a cold morning to do the milking—I was sitting on a little stool beside the cow and had put a cloth over my legs so I wouldn't wet my pants with milk, the child still crying.

After that night I started taking every precaution: when I was about to cum I'd pull my dick out from inside Amália and cum on her stomach, just like in porn flicks, the guy ejaculating outside the woman, who then rubbed herself with cum and in some cases licked it.

Other times I preferred Amália from behind— it was more relaxed because I didn't need to worry that as soon as I got to the edge I'd have to pull out, and Amália had started to like it more and more when I did her from behind, telling me she'd never done it that way before, but then it became frequent that in the middle of our caresses she'd turn over and ask me to get inside her.

She never breathed another word about a child.

I don't know if any of the other residents at the manor found out about my nocturnal absences. One morning as I was returning from one of my encounters with Amália, I ran into Otávio, seated at the kitchen table drinking, pulling hard from a bottle of gin. I sat in front of him and looked at his bulky features, his sometimes jowly habit of chewing on nothing, as if ruminating on some gory predilection that prohibited mention—Kurt and Gerda seemed to prefer things left unsaid, the intervals—so that he was obliged to remain there, turning things over, turning that strength, perhaps already useless, deteriorated, between what remained of his teeth.

But when I sat down he stopped chewing, looked at me, and said:

"It was always like that."

"What's that, Otávio?" I asked.

"Like that…"

"What?" I insisted.

Otávio, without stopping:

"Ever since I saw him for the first time, riding his horse, when he looked at me half-cockeyed from above and asked if I wanted work, ever since then I've become his trained bloodhound, the one that tries things first, to save his master from falling into any traps, so on any trip, in any unknown place, if he thought the smell of the food was off, he'd ask me to take the first forkful and see if everything was all right, same with women, some of them I've tasted first, before him, like wine; it was the fear that poison could be hidden anywhere, so I tried first—this lethal mistrust always afflicted him, he kept me fed and housed to try to cure it, he took me on some trips, never once let me off my leash."

The next morning, on one of my walks, I once again happened upon Kurt and Otávio going at it. I watched from behind a tree, only this time everything looked worse: there came a moment when, with a blow to the chin, Kurt fell and didn't get up. Otávio hovered around Kurt for a bit, then finally decided to drag him by the legs back to the manor.

Kurt disappeared for a few days, at meals Gerda would say that it was another attack of the flu, the beginnings of bronchitis, but later she'd just enter in total silence.

During Kurt's long disappearance, Otávio barely touched his food, staring fixedly at a photograph beside the window, blotted by patina: a little naked child, lying on its stomach.

Never before those days had I felt so acutely the monotony of the noises plates and silverware make at mealtime. I kept wondering whether, if Kurt never came back, they would still let me live on the estate, comfortable, without a care, as things had been until then.

I awoke to a gorgeous Saturday, and the first sound I heard when I woke up was Kurt's voice. I went quickly to the hallway, the door of the couple's room was open, Kurt was saying that the stock market was down, he needed to call Miguel, Gerda told him that on TV they said that the depression was just transitory—that was when I heard steps and went back to my room.

I had affixed to the wall of my room an image that appeared nothing like the one I imagined when I first arrived at the manor: I'd recently found an old engraving in Amália's shed, rolled up in a corner, yellowed in spots, likely by the drops of rain that came in through the slats, depicting a boat setting sail. It was signed by the name of Wilhelm Müller.

Kurt let me hang it up.

"That engraving evokes, with impressive realism, a farewell to one's homeland," he said, as if half asleep.

The poem I was writing then spoke of a farewell, and in that farewell exploded a hatred that tore through everything: ripped curtains, the walls to sawdust, blood on the lapel. Something was missing at the end of the poem that for three days I labored in vain to find.

In a little while, I'd have breakfast, and hoped Kurt would be there, for no other reason than to feel secure. I thought that to keep up my form I'd need to believe with more conviction every day that Kurt was my protector.

At breakfast Kurt was occupying his place at

the table, he had his right arm in a sling, and sometimes Gerda leaned over to help him raise his cup to
his lips.

Otávio was talking a lot, recalling that the an-
niversary of his return to Brazil from the war was
approaching.

"It was a day like this, sunny," he mentioned,
staring at the pattern on the tablecloth.

Amália was making her rounds of the table,
asking if anybody needed anything, dissembling
and stealing chances to wink at me furtively—the
night before she'd remained for hours sitting on the
ground, leaning against the bed: it was raining, there
was a leak, the whole shed damp, and Amália, nude
above the waist, told me that Gerda had cancer, she
and Kurt had already gone to Rio de Janeiro a few
times to see a famous doctor, one time Gerda stayed
there for weeks, checked into a clinic, I told Amália
that out here with her I didn't want to hear anything
about illness, and I went to her and started licking
her breasts, sucking, started unbuttoning my pants,
asked her to touch me, and she touched me, a drop
of rain got through the shaft in the roof and wet my

nose, I was about to cum in her hand, her breasts seemed very full, swollen, I was afraid she was pregnant, but my dread lasted only a second, and then I returned to sucking and biting her two breasts, because I remembered it had been a long time since I came inside her, so I could keep on sucking and biting her two breasts with peace of mind, the rain drumming on the zinc way up high, and suddenly Amália let out a yell, and shouted, murderer, murderer, twice, and I, who was wrapped in her arms, got up, took her hand, and saw deep in her eyes a sign of alarm, but concluded that I didn't feel like deciphering it.

I passed Kurt in the hallway, and for the first time he showed me a real smile. What's happening? I wondered, what am I doing that could make him so decisively happy?

I left the manor and went through the surrounding fields, racking my brains to see if I could understand that smile: What trait of mine could bring such a pleasured look to his eye? I needed to discover what it was so I could broaden my access to this strange benefactor.

I sat on the highest part of the low hill and looked down to see Amália throwing things on an enormous fire—papers, cardboard boxes, wood, broken springs—it was making a lot of smoke, and I got down low so that she wouldn't be able to see me.

I stayed there, lying on my belly in the tall grass, hidden in a war trench, daydreaming that I was entering an unknown world, and that to remain in it I'd need skills.

The strong burning smell left me a little stupid, and into my head leaped the hypothesis that Kurt had set me up, that he'd never give anything up. I turned my belly to the sky, exhaled slowly. Overhead, an airplane was heading south.

Days later I wrote a whole poem in one sitting called "Scenes of War"—the distant stamping, surrounding quake, a hemorrhage running from the nostrils of a boy as he woke.

The poem, written on that paper...even if I slipped away, the poem would still be there, and I thought about how they gave me very little to do besides write poems, and that, until that day, I hadn't really determined anything about my new situation—in that huge house, surrounded by fields.

Someone knocked on the door. I got up and opened it, it was Kurt, he asked to come in, I felt weak in the knees: perhaps now I would learn the worst of it.

Kurt stepped in slowly, went up to my desk, looked over it, brought his hand to rest on the dark wood, stroking it, letting his head fall gently, his voice low:

"You're coming with me and Gerda, we're going to Rio de Janeiro, Gerda is sick, she's going to check into a hospital in Rio for a while, for observation. If she doesn't need more intense treatment this time, the three of us will go to Germany. Gerda has some things to attend to in Berlin."

My head spun.

"Yes," I remembered to say.

The next morning I went with Kurt to apply for a passport in Porto Alegre. I'd forgotten that the manor wasn't far from the city. We got there in a little more than an hour.

After we took care of the passport we walked around a bit downtown. When we passed by the

door of the Sulacap Building, on Borges, Kurt
stopped, made an expression like he'd remembered
something, said he had to make a quick visit to a
friend's office, that we'd meet up again in an hour
at the McDonald's on Alfândega Square. Then he
took his wallet from the inside pocket of his jacket
and gave me money. I stood there watching as he
entered the Sulacap Building.

I started walking again, lazily, without feeling
like it, as if Porto Alegre no longer interested me. If
only there were a way for me to remain in Rio per-
manently, or even in Germany, in Europe, without
losing the setup Kurt had provided me.

I perused the same used bookstores as always,
looking at everything reluctantly, I couldn't avoid
grimacing at the gazes that crossed with mine, somebody walked by staring at me, I cussed, he stopped,
he yelled for me to be a man and repeat what I'd
said, curious bystanders surrounded us, just a luna-
tic in my way I said, and turned and made my way
through all those people, the guy looked like he was
about to punch me in the back but hands reached
out to stop him, I saw him held back by a thousand

arms, staring at me with his shirt all unbuttoned, panting, red, hair strewn across his forehead.

People at McDonald's were noisy. I tapped my foot to the tacky music that was playing softly, preferring to make an effort to listen and follow the music than to sit there listening to conversations that made me want to pick another fight: Kurt was ten minutes late, and when he arrived I took a deep breath and got up without realizing it, I asked what he wanted, and he said just a Coke, and when I came back with the Coke Kurt was smiling and completely absorbed by watching me. As I sat down I forced a smile to go along with his—my smile was half crooked and I let it fall, but since Kurt kept smiling, still rapt, I tried again, but this time what came out was a cackle that you could hear thirty yards away, and Kurt looked at me and let out a coarse laugh—he had perfect enameled teeth, dentures or maybe implants, and Kurt was much older, older than I could tell before. Otávio still had a certain stiffness to his face, Gerda looked like she'd had a little work done, but Kurt, this man laughing his low laugh right here in my face, he was the one who looked the oldest of the three, and he laughed, and I laughed, and we kept at it for a while in that McDonald's.

When Kurt's thin lips finally closed, I concluded that never again would I see him laugh so effusively, I could barely believe how genuine his laughter had been—I wondered if he hadn't had a fit of hysteria or something—and as the car descended the parking garage ramps the mood that came over us was the same one as always, reserved, sometimes bored, other times not, a silence from which a verse might spring, like in the car now, with Bach on the stereo, a lumberjack having a nap, holding the ax against his chest like a child.

I looked sidelong, examined Kurt's profile, and without being able to contain it I let out a silent but stinky fart. I rolled down the window, said that the temperature wasn't so bad, though the wind blowing against my ear was super cold—maybe Kurt hadn't even noticed the smell, he seemed to be listening to the chorale, enjoying his German choral music. For my part I had no complaints, I was going to put up the window as soon as the smell went away, and then I'd pretend to rest my eyes, take a nap, dream that I was in Rio, or in Berlin, or maybe even Amsterdam.

I was awakened by Kurt's voice calling me. In front of us was a huge line of stopped trucks with people piled on top of them. Farther ahead was a beautiful sunset, the teeth of a rake held up against the light. I rubbed my eyes, Kurt told me they were landless people who wanted to occupy a farm that was up around the next curve.

A soldier holding a pistol appeared. He leaned into the car on Kurt's side, said there were a bunch of encampments already on the farm, but the Brigade had intercepted more than half of them—those who were in the trucks in front of us wouldn't advance any farther.

The soldier told us we could drive along the shoulder.

Kurt started to drive along the shoulder, the car passing by those people perched on top of the trucks, crying children, a pregnant woman holding her belly, placards asking for a plot of land, settlement, agrarian reform. The car went along with some difficulty over holes and muddy patches, but as though to compensate, the landless people didn't say a word to us, good or bad, and getting through them didn't take long since we were already close to home.

Amália had once again thrown some junk on a fire—with a piece of wood she went about stirring it into the flame: a chair with a partial backrest and missing a leg was beside her, waiting its turn. I thought about whistling from the car, giving her a sign, but for the past few days Amália wouldn't even look at me, lowering her eyes when she passed by, and I actually felt relieved that the thing with her had ended this way, without any effort on my part.

As Kurt parked, three huge dogs I'd never seen before ran up to the car, barking out their fury— one of them put its paws against my window. Kurt told me that in situations like this Otávio let the dogs loose. He asked me not to get out for now, then went in front of the car and started to scold the animals in German—slowly the dogs stopped barking and sat down around Kurt. He signaled for me to get out.

Otávio was on the porch, in a straw chair with a

wide back, his hands nervously trying to cover a gun resting in his lap, he didn't want to look at me as I went by.

I went to my room, night had already fallen, and up the road the landless people were striking matches, a pitiful flame would extinguish and then another would light up nearby. I leaned out the window and remembered a song that kids used to sing back in my Glória days, but I couldn't get past the first verse, and even that single verse began to dilute in my head and came undone within minutes—it actually seemed like suddenly my destiny had overtaken me, along with all the songs that used to flow from my lips by heart, such that there would come a time when I'd look back and wouldn't be able to recognize anything. Soon I'll no longer need to lift a finger to evade my past, I thought with relief.

The dogs were perturbed, they wouldn't stop barking, and I threw myself in bed with a deep fear of finding myself outside this situation which provided me a bed and everything else.

I rolled around on the mattress for hours on end—I found it strange they hadn't called me to supper—the dogs were quiet now, but they weren't sleeping, I could hear them pacing nearby, the cavernous respiration of beasts, a voice from up on the highway, certainly someone transmitting a warning across the distance, others responded, every now and then a child's cry, then suddenly a shout, but this shout had come from the manor, and it was a woman's, it was Gerda's, and someone knocked on my door, Kurt asking me for help, Gerda was lying on the bed breathing with difficulty, Kurt said he was going to open up her nightgown a little, to alleviate the feeling of asphyxiation, and he opened the nightgown, and from between her shriveled breasts to beneath her navel was an ugly cut, and Kurt asked me to help him carry her to the armchair, I said I could do it myself, and I took Gerda in my arms, and as I carried her she put her arms around my neck and began to hiccup, I stopped, saw through the window in front of me that they were still lighting matches up on the highway, only now there were fewer flames flaring and extinguishing, and Gerda hiccupped while clasped to my neck, Kurt pointed to the armchair, I put her there, she wiped her hands across her eyes, stopped hiccupping.

The dogs had begun to bark again.

I went to the kitchen for a drink of water and found Otávio, who was seated with his hands on the table, a glass tipped over, a bottle of red wine without a label. I brought a glass of water to the table and sat down in front of him.

"So, Otávio?" I attempted.

He coughed, said that he was going back to his homeland, Jaguarão, to stay with his elderly mother—she couldn't live by herself anymore, and he was tired of it here.

A few days went by in a downpour of rain, the landless wouldn't budge from the highway. Sometimes troops of military police would get down from the Brigade trucks in nylon slickers that came almost down to their feet and stand there talking with a group of occupiers—one afternoon a lightning bolt struck nearby, rumbling everything, but it caused only a few shouts to ring out, children bawling, coughing, they must be drenched to the bone—my trip with Kurt and Gerda never materialized, I thought, because of the stalemate with the landless people practically on our doorstep.

After the thunderbolt, in the middle of all the commotion, I noticed that some of the children were slipping through the wire fence and running down to Amália's shed. A lot of kids had gone in, and it surprised me that there wasn't any noise coming from down there, as though when they entered the shed they lost their tongues or fainted or maybe made a pact of silence, the fact is that it intrigued me, and I decided to go take a look.

It was late afternoon, rather dark in the shed, a slew of completely mute children surrounded Amália: she was sitting on the bed, indifferent to a fly on her neck, another on her arm—near the lit candle, her face was awash in deathlike clarity and from her eyes ran tears, many tears. The children contemplated her.

I remained there only a short while. I'm certain Amália didn't see me.

The next day the landless people left the highway; it seemed like they had gone far away.

That same day Amália disappeared. Otávio said he'd heard she followed the squatters' caravan.

Now I was sitting on the toilet, elbows to

knees, looking out at what the doorframe let me
see of the rest of my hotel room in Rio. Kurt
still hadn't set foot in the room, he never left the
hospital he'd checked Gerda into—I'd taken him
changes of clothes many times. Whenever I went
to the hospital Gerda didn't look very good lying
there in bed, often she was taken out in a wheel-
chair for new tests, but now I was sitting on the
toilet, looking at what the open door showed me
of my hotel room, and there, like that, I could only
think that once again everything seemed like a
figment of my imagination: I, who had never even
been on an airplane, had gone first class, Kurt and
I on either side of Gerda, our feet resting on cush-
ions, and after getting to Rio, had checked into this
hotel near Leme, a room all to myself, for me who
had never before stayed in any hotel, not even the
lousiest kind—I was now looking at a hotel room
where I could stay all day if I liked, watching TV,
reading, scratching my balls, sleeping, though I'd
rather spend the time walking around Copacabana,
Ipanema, I wanted to get to know the city and was
eager because later there would be other cities in

Germany, Europe—and so I got up, flushed the toilet, and decided to trim the beard that had grown ever since my time at the clinic in São Leopoldo. With the sound of each snip of the scissors I repeated a sort of mantra, a sound that I'd never be able to remember later, but that seemed right then to have been mine since the womb, and I repeated it in front of the mirror, with my face, little by little, stripped of the beard that fell in lockets into the sink, and repeating it brought back my confidence: what was being given to me would be mine forever, it was only a matter of getting used to the silence of my reasons for being there and no longer a squatter in a crummy apartment building, everything would be fine, and for this reason I repeated my mantra and smoothed my face once more in preparation for the rest, which would be even better.

I ran a hand over my chin, summoned the elevator, the uniformed operator asked me smilingly which floor—everyone was smiling at me in that four-star joint—I remembered I wanted to have a whiskey in the hotel bar, asked for the first floor, the bartender treated me like a prince, yeah, I shaved,

I told him, also smiling, a whiskey poured over the stones in my glass, and the bartender was saying he hadn't recognized me with my face like a baby's bottom, then turned back to the same chatter as always, recommending where to go later, at night, beaches, bars, women, I barely followed what he was saying, but it pleased me to confirm that someone behind the bar was capable of busying himself with my day's itinerary just because I had the money to pay for the hotel and leave tips. I was discovering that it pleased me to pay for the world's courtesies.

In the middle of the afternoon, I left to walk down Nossa Senhora da Copacabana. I stopped in front of a movie poster—there wasn't much else to do—I entered, and in the cinema bathroom there were a few men standing around smoking. I started to take a piss—all the urinals were occupied and I could sense the eyes of the men standing there in urinating position were directed at me. I figured out what was happening: nobody was urinating here, they all had their dicks out but were staring at my dick, all of them middle-aged, the smell of urine ferocious, from the cinema came an uproar that must have been a violent car crash, the screech of brakes, and in front of the urinals those eyes wouldn't stop staring at my dick, and when I looked down again I saw that it wasn't pissing anymore and, without my having noticed, had gotten completely hard— someone tapped my shoulder, I turned, it was a guy behind me reaching his hand inside a greasy jacket at chest height, he said he was a cop and wanted to see my ID, working papers too—I was getting dragged out from my situation under Kurt's wing: if I got thrown in jail again he'd never give me another chance and I'd find myself face-to-face with complete shit all over again, this time with two arrests—I put my instantly slackened dick back in my pants as the guy tried to act high and mighty, demanding my working papers again, the faggots all around were dying with laughter. I realized that I'd been ambushed, and as I zipped up I remembered that I had very little money with me and that it wasn't likely I could strike a deal with the guy who said he was a cop—then a plan for escape suddenly sprang up inside me, I didn't even have time to think it through before I'd already begun to execute it, my whole body collapsing onto the cold, piss-drenched floor, trembling from an attack that made me drool: dig my fingernails into the air, break out in a sweat, roll back my eyes until I could no longer see anything around me, all stiff, in my vision just dark and muddled shapes that I tried to break open with sweeping arms, like I was swimming breaststroke—I wanted to scream but couldn't find my voice, flailing in the middle of those dark and muddled shapes, in vain, my strength having failed—a giant drain slowly swallowing me.

Suddenly my body calmed, normalizing my breathing. I didn't understand what I was doing there, lying with my head in a puddle of piss, deeply inhaling the sharp smell of piss, as though predicting this would help me recover my memory, and the memory that had knocked me to the floor appeared, little by little, and I became fascinated, as what had begun as a theatrical seizure to get rid of the guy who called himself a cop had become a thing that had really thrown me outside myself.

And now I was returning, with a tremendous vertigo, incapable of understanding anything further: Who was this man helping me get up, picking me up by the arm and guiding me slowly, as slow as two insects going against the immensity of the others? Who was this man who guided me finally to a mirror, a mirror that didn't verify my features or those of the atmosphere around me—didn't permit me to know if I was still in the same place? Who was this man who continued to hold my arm and was asking me to splash my forehead and come with him, that he'd take me wherever I needed to go?...

Then, on the sidewalk outside the hotel, standing up straight again, touching the man's shoulder, telling him something for the first time, saying goodbye, thanking him.

I wrapped myself in a towel and went to the hotel steam room. Kurt was there, seated, his head hanging toward his feet.

I came close and waved my hand in front of my face, trying to make a clearing in the steam: Kurt had gotten even older, I could see that now. How? I wondered, and shook my head without understanding this strange dose of aging. Hmm…since when?

He still hadn't seen me, just a few feet away,

wrapped in his mists.

Suddenly he saw me. I had the urge to retreat, to hide myself amid the steam.

I'm exhausted, he said. Tonight I'll sleep at the hotel. I need you to stay at the hospital with Gerda. You should go soon, he concluded, and returned his gaze to the direction of his feet, absorbed in his thoughts.

I switched on the lamp, and saw Gerda sleeping, her breath blowing a few strands of blue hair near her lip. I swallowed a lump in my throat, not because of Gerda's condition, but because I abruptly discerned how indefensible my presence there was: What was I doing in a Rio hospital room, beside a sick and practically unknown woman?

Wouldn't it be better to leave the room and try to forget about the existence of Kurt and Gerda, and find some less blind situation, one as clear as my hand, which opened like a fan in front of the lamp-shade, my fingers the succinct verses I'd like to have?

But there was Gerda, under my care.

I touched the hand on the white sheet covering her, and she opened her eyes. She closed them again.

I opened the blinds. On the other side of the street was an abandoned lot. I felt a shiver, like something was about to happen, and went to see if Gerda needed anything from me.

It looked like she had touched up the dye job on her hair with a shade closer to purple. I noticed that she'd aged like Kurt had recently. How much time had passed? I asked myself this question as I watched shadows on the wall, making me drowsy.

Once more I put my hand on the sheet that covered her. Gerda opened her eyes again. I saw that they were very red, watery. She gazed at the ceiling for a few minutes—it took her a while to notice my presence.

Suddenly she suffered a shudder of pain, and then she saw me. I half smiled, not exactly because I felt obliged to force an air of consolation in front of a sick person, but because I barely knew Gerda, just as I barely knew anything in my life after the Glória neighborhood back in Porto Alegre, and aside from that, Gerda made me feel an embarrassment beyond what I was used to feeling around Kurt, and her presence seemed to demand a more ceremonious expression, because she was so quiet, distant, mysterious.

But that night Gerda was different: when she saw me a wide smile broke across her face, and I could see just how white her teeth were, and then she started talking, far more than I would have expected from her.

She asked me what time it was and how long she'd been there. I told her the time, and then confessed that I didn't really know how long she'd been in the hospital—I'd think about it—I just knew that Kurt had given me the task of keeping her company that night.

Ah, Kurt, Gerda said to me, Kurt… She looked at me, without losing her smile, and at that moment I realized that the Gerda lying there wasn't the one I knew, a decidedly different woman occupied Gerda's body now, another woman who allowed herself to flourish in front of me for the first time, or maybe not, maybe Gerda was deliriously ill, but I didn't want to call anyone, not the floor physician, not the nurses—I let her take my hand and sigh, Kurt, ah Kurt, she was speaking with such an enthusiastic tone, perhaps beyond what was appropriate—I knew nothing or next to nothing about the state of Gerda's health beyond the cancer Amália told me about and the immense scar I saw cutting across her thorax—but at that moment Gerda seemed to come to the surface of whatever ailment was afflicting her, and told me that it was in Hamburg after the war that the two of them met, that they'd both been born and raised in Brazil by German parents, and in Hamburg they danced away the night, they would dance and the most foolish words would come to their lips—Gerda was sweating, her voice breathless, she was sweating a lot and holding my hand between hers, staring at me and repeating pained, choppy sentences with Kurt's name.

She remembered how as soon as they met they came back to Brazil—Gerda's father owned the land where they still lived today, they'd built a house there, married, but children never came, and what she had inside herself began to hurt, like a land that was cultivated in her mind but would re-main always and forever unknown.

No, I said, not an always and forever unknown

country, I answered, as a way to prevent Gerda from succumbing to a memory that seemed to be making things worse, since, at the moment she said the words *always and forever unknown country*, I perceived—right when in the middle of it she had given a long pause and gasped—it was just then that everything started to seem very serious, even though she was able to keep going and continued to hold my hand all by herself, she was even pulling my hand, yes, such that I was being pulled, dragged out of myself, lying on top of her body as I was doing now and devouring her, and when she said my God, a spasm, in a flash her body slackened, wilted, para-lyzed, but not mine, mine was still going, and then came to the climax with a heaving gasp, to the point of evanescing over that woman who was no longer reacting, a stone.

It took me a while to untangle myself from Gerda's inert arms. I didn't feel the need to close her eyes, went into the bathroom.

As I urinated, trying to focus on and destroy a small fleck of filth that seemed to be crusted onto the white porcelain of the toilet, a nurse came into the room and announced that she was going to give Gerda an injection, and that with this dose she'd be in sufficient condition to get on a plane to Germany in a few days.

I went to the door of the bathroom, still zipping my fly. The nurse gave a few hysterical little laughs with the stuff for the injection in her hand, and started to tell me that Gerda was recovering all her functions nicely: she was going to the bathroom religiously at bedtime, after her dinner had settled, and no longer felt pain during her bowel movements.

She won't be having any more bowel movements, I told her. Huh? the nurse probed. Look, I said, pointing to Gerda's body.

I lifted Gerda's hand, raised my index finger to her wrist, and her pulse beat twice, three times. I released her hand somewhat brusquely, stepped away. The nurse explained that this response from a dead body could last for a few hours. I asked her to close Gerda's eyes, I'd already had enough of that still-warm death.

The nurse went out, I went to the window.

The sun was trying to come out. In the vacant lot out front were five ragamuffin drifters, all of them standing with expectant posture, staring insistently at me. What did they want from me? I wondered, and lowered the blinds.

I picked up the phone and dialed the number of the hotel. She died, I said to Kurt. He said he'd come over later.

Nearby, a flock of birds started to sing. I lay down on the sofa, closed my eyes.

I opened my eyes, guessing the steps in the hallway were Kurt's. This at least I recognized, Kurt's gait. Before he opened the door I got up and went over to Gerda's body. Kurt came close. He said he'd already brought our bags, he'd left them with the hospital doorman.

Only then did I notice that Gerda was ready, dressed in a gray skirt suit and white blouse, her half-open mouth lipsticked a pale pink, cotton in her nostrils.

I thought: how long will the funeral last? Through the slits in the blinds, I could see it was a clear day.

I looked at Kurt, but there was nothing to read on his face but fatigue. I turned my eyes back to the bright slits in the blinds and couldn't stop thinking about the trip to Germany, certain to be canceled now.

We'll take the body to Porto Alegre this morning, Kurt said.

And a horrible alarm clock began to go off inside the closet. As Kurt opened the closet the alarm shut off.

A shot in the yard out front. That was the first line of a poem I wrote in its entirety on the spot. I kept the poem in my head all the way to the airport. When we got there, I sat down at a lunch counter and copied it onto a paper napkin. It was the last poem I wrote. After that I never wrote another poem again.

But for the time being I was still standing there, composing the poem, the words coming in streams, in front of me was Gerda's body, and just beyond was Kurt, standing to face me. He was staring at me. A shot in the yard out front / A hardened fingernail scraping the tepid earth—that's how the poem continued, and to remember it I'd kept repeating it in my head line by line while I waited until it was time to escape that foul-smelling hospital room.

Gerda's casket was put in a special car, half-chromed—Kurt and I were in front of the hospital waiting for a taxi to take us to the airport. We wouldn't see the casket again until Porto Alegre.

When Kurt bent down to get into the taxi, I had an urge to help him but I stopped, as though preferring to closely watch what I was seeing: this man had really aged beyond his years, he was getting into the taxi with such difficulty that it left my mouth agape, thinking about how unprepared I was to track the passage of time.

It's that Kurt had practically turned into an old man—and I, if I stopped to take note, would no doubt find myself a man and not the boy that Kurt pulled out of jail.

A period had passed since the day Kurt brought me to be with him, and now there was no denying it: this period had been longer than I had supposed.

And I wondered, a wave of goosebumps passing over the flesh of my scalp: Why this lapse in recognizing such a duration?

In any case, if I managed somehow to cure this lapse, if my memory ran backward to reconstruct this time, who would be able to evaluate its accuracy?

Something happened, I said to myself, and the secret seems to have been lost inside me, or maybe there, inside Kurt, a man unshaken by tears or any sort of commotion. And there he was, sitting in the backseat of the taxi, waiting for me to get in and remain beside his infinite dryness until we got to the airport, then from one airport to another, and from there to the manor for who knows how many more years, and from the manor, finally, to the edge of a hole—certainly the same as Gerda's.

I sat beside Kurt. Gerda's casket had already gone on ahead—it would obviously get crammed deep into the entrails of the airplane so that none of the passengers would see it.

As the taxi drove along Guanabara Bay, Kurt raised his hand in a tremulous gesture, and recalled that, years ago, he had come to Rio on business by himself a few times, in those days he stayed at the Copacabana Palace, he had an old friend who lived in Rio, younger than him, heir to a large fortune, who later died of leukemia—at the mention of the friend's death I looked over at Kurt, he was taking pains to hold his gaze, looking out over Guanabara Bay—this friend had taken him for nights out on the town in Rio, in his company Kurt had even drank cachaça, until then he'd never tasted it, but it wasn't pure cachaça, it was mixed with Coke, and this mixture was called samba-in-Berlin, samba-in-Berlin was what we ordered in the good old days, Kurt was saying carefully, without registering any emotion, the strange thing was that he started repeating the story of his trips to Rio: the friend, heir to a solid fortune, the two of them in the arbor at the Copacabana Palace, a world-famous actress whose name he'd now forgotten surrounded by photographers, and the story would stop when he got to that mixture of cachaça and Coke, the samba-in-Berlin, then he started over, repeating what he'd said before—those trips to Rio, the heir friend—always adding a detail or two, the late afternoon on the beach at Urca, the window of his hotel room facing the beach, and of course, topping it all off was the samba-in-Berlin—three, four, five times, as though he were trying to illuminate a point that kept escaping him, making it necessary to start all over again, two, three more times, and so on, until we arrived at Galeão airport and Kurt finally stanched the flow of his memories. His last phrase:

"The samba-in-Berlin went down harsh."

Well, I won't be seeing Berlin this time, I reflected as Kurt passed some bills to the cabbie. But I need to man up, was what I whispered into my shirt collar, turning to see Rio for the last time, an arm's length away from the open airport door.

I took the napkin from that airport lunch counter and started to take down the poem, tapping on the bar with my fingers to the rhythm of the last lines I'd put on paper: A shot in the yard out front / A hardened fingernail scraping the tepid earth—and I went on like that for six or seven more lines.

On the plane, the only open seats were separate from each other. I sat down and took a deep breath. Poor Kurt, I thought as the plane took off, poor everyone who had such a heavy burden. Kurt slept the whole way, seated three rows in front of me.

About halfway through the flight, with my tray all messy and up against my chest, a glass of wine washing down my dessert, the flight attendant passed and smiled at me, and since we were going through some turbulence I gave her a bit of a yellow smile. When she passed by again maybe I would tell her I wrote poems—the start of a conversation that might interest her in me, since I ought to have kept in mind that I was no longer a young boy, but a man in the fullness of my functions in need of a woman to keep me company—Kurt would need to give his blessing to this union, preferably with a blonde girl like Gerda seemed she'd once been, he'd be so satisfied he'd give me half his fortune, opening the way not only to Germany but to who knows what other quadrants, and once I'd divorced the dumb blonde, a different woman in every hotel room.

While we were waiting for our bags near the escalator in the Porto Alegre airport, I looked out the window onto the runway and saw our plane disgorge Gerda's casket from the lower compartment of the plane, near the tail—the chestnut coffin was lowered down with ropes, as if it were being birthed from the entrails of some gigantic animal, the coffin, and inside it Gerda, whom I'd savagely bitten the night before—I don't know if the person who washed and dressed her noticed the marks my teeth left on I don't remember what part of her body, all I know is that she moaned, cried, seconds later shouted, My God, looked me in the eye for the first time, deeply, then died.

Across the runway, two men were pushing a sort of litter onto which they'd place the coffin.

It was a sunny day, just one or two clouds.

A man in a white jumpsuit was coming down the runway, obviously some sort of airport official, he looked at me and seemed to understand, because he closed his eyes when he saw me, then threw his glance to the side, as though he'd already seen enough—I could still see that his expression had turned a bit nauseated, and when he looked in my direction again his gaze looked numbed, refusing to see.

The late afternoon shadows had already insinuated themselves among the branches of the Protestant cemetery, the discreet headstones engraved almost exclusively with German names. Kurt and I were walking down a path and our steps made a cadence on the flagstones. Ahead of us, a gravedigger was pushing a little cart that carried Gerda's casket. The wheels could've used an oiling, they made an infernal noise. From time to time the vision of an iron cross, stark, made my head pulse. Gerda's grave just wouldn't arrive. The gravedigger was really putting an effort into pushing the little cart, steeply bent over, his ass sticking out at us, pants straining at the seam between his enormous buttocks. I noticed it was getting darker. And the gravedigger started down another path.

At that time of day it was hard to discern the bottom of the grave. The gravedigger asked Kurt if he'd like to open the casket one last time. Kurt shook his head no, and nearby a bell began to toll.

I threw a shovelful of earth into the hole.

We caught a taxi right there on what they called the melancholy hill, the city lights shining below, passing down the avenue with grave after grave on both sides of the road, I remembered the times I'd spend whole days up there, back when I lived in the

Glória squat. All that seemed to have ended a long time ago, so long, but at the same time the memory galled me, made me want to vomit, stick my finger down my throat and expel all that detritus from my memory.

Our arrival at the manor.

The power was out. We lit lanterns.

I found a horrible bug underneath the stove. It could have been a spider but it looked more like a hangman. I was on my knees and I smashed it with the base of my lantern. The moon was full. The low sky, clotted with stars, was coming in the kitchen window. December, but the night couldn't be called warm—because it was windy. I was crawling along the kitchen tiles with lantern in hand, looking for something that Kurt couldn't find. I was crawling across the kitchen without much hope for my search: he didn't have the faintest idea of where I could find it. It was a December night, bright, so bright that I almost didn't need a lantern.

I knocked three times on the half-open door to Kurt's room. I still had the lantern in my hand. In Kurt's room there was another lantern. The lantern in Kurt's room was on top of the nightstand. Kurt thanked me, said he'd already found what he was looking for. Do you need anything else? I asked. He said no, he didn't need anything, he was going to sleep. If you need anything just give a shout, I said to the outline of his face.

The night was also entering through my bedroom window. Kurt didn't just listen to Bach in the car, he liked to hear Bach all day long, preferably while closed up in his room. That night he couldn't listen to Bach because the power was out. The truck with no muffler passing by on the road belonged to a guy I knew, the son of the owner of a small farm on the other side of the tall hill. One time he rolled the truck nearby and messed up his leg. Of all the stars that one is the brightest, my eyes tear up when I face it, like now. Kurt's already snoring. The power's back on.

I pick up the radio, pull the antenna way up. I turn out the light, lie down with the radio on my chest. I hear noises, interferences, spin the dial this way and that, voices from all over the world: a show in Portuguese coming from Moscow, Asian languages, French, English, German. One among the voices catches my attention, it speaks in Spanish and says: if you can hear me don't change the station, stay where you are, keep everything intact and I'll arrive in seconds to remake you, you will become another. Then comes a sort of ethereal music, the half-open door creaks like someone is pushing it, trying to get in, and the hand that's now touching my arm suppresses me, and I know that I should annul myself in this way, without sorrow, so that another can come and take my place, I no longer exist here, I lack.

I awoke in the morning clutching the radio to my chest, low music badly tuned in. In the mirror I saw that during the night a zit had formed above my eyebrow. Big, very red and inflamed. The first thought I had was if Kurt had brought Gerda's things from Rio—what I wanted to know: if I could find her makeup things, foundation, that's what women call the flesh-toned paste I needed to see if I could find to blot out my zit.

Kurt was listening to Bach in his room. From six a.m. onward, he began to move implacably through his morning routine. So Kurt was in his room listening to Bach. I knocked three times on the closed door. He opened. I saw there was a woman inside with her back to the door. Leaning against the wall, looking down, like someone who felt sad, or maybe embarrassed—but from the thick black hair that fell down her shoulders and the way her left foot was resting on her right knee I had no doubts—is that Amália? I asked, and only later realized I'd pried into something before confirming what it was. Kurt said nothing—she turned and I saw her, fatter, her hips much wider—who knows where this penniless woman could have gone to return so corpulent, having left here a petite girl, almost unsatisfying, now returning so full of flesh.

"Hi, Amália."

"Hi…"

Then I took hold of a finger on my left hand, raised an eyebrow, and told Kurt that I'd hurt my finger opening a window, asked if I could get the mercurochrome from the bathroom in his room (something I sometimes did). Kurt nodded yes and asked Amália to make him some coffee and see if the cow was still giving milk. And the two went out.

I opened the bathroom closet, rummaged around, ended up finding the foundation. With my usual tendency to overdo it, I plastered my forehead with foundation. Now no one would ever imagine I had that damn zit.

I went to find Amália. Not because her now-opulent flesh made her newly appealing in my eyes, nothing like that. It's that a curiosity was gnawing me: to know what had happened to her, where she'd gone, with whom.

Amália was trying to milk a cow that recalled one of those animals decaying on drought-scorched earth.

"Where were you?" I asked.

"I went crazy for one of the landless squatters, I followed him. I ended up pregnant, ran away, got bigger and bigger, so swollen that one day as I went through a little village I stopped in the pharmacy to weigh myself: two hundred and fifty-three pounds. I was ready to pop. I looked for my sister and found her right where I suspected, twenty miles away— she pulled the thing from my belly faster than I could have imagined—I didn't stick around long, I ran away through the countryside with that thing in my arms and drowned it in the first river I came to. They caught me, imprisoned me, now I'm here."

"So then a long time really has gone by." I affected fright, as though I was only then discovering it, at that instant.

I ran my fingers through the thick paste of sweaty foundation that was almost running into my eye.

"And the milk?" I asked.

"The milk won't come out." Amália yanked the cow's teats and made a strong expression of either rage or repugnance.

Then the cow tottered, tottered, tried to take a few steps, fell back, collapsed, and upon collapsing, its bones made a muffled noise, as though there were soundproof glass between me and what I was watching.

"Bye, Amália," I said.

As I neared the manor I saw the shape of a man on the porch, I could tell he was knocking on the door, a small suitcase at his feet—I saw Kurt open the door, the man entering, running his hand through his gray hair, and when the man ran his hand through his hair I understood it was Otávio with his old habit of running his hand through his grizzled hair.

First Amália, now Otávio: they're coming back, I thought, they don't know how to live out from under Kurt's wing, they tried to extricate themselves but came right back to the center of what they never should have left.

And I, was I not another of Kurt's charges? I couldn't forget that he was already old, I didn't have much time to get myself together and avoid ending up like the other two, stripped of everything that I'd managed to remake, far from here.

"How's your mother, Otávio?" I asked, taking his cold hand.

"She died, just like Gerda died."

Otávio was wearing a panicked expression. He'd transformed into a worn-out old man, a lump, larger than an avocado, had formed on the back of his head. He could barely turn his head, and when he tried he grimaced horribly in pain.

That afternoon I thought about appealing to Kurt's heart, always so impassive, even with me, whom he seemed to hold in a certain esteem. So I invited Otávio to get some fresh air with me—he came along, and we went for a walk, he with a gimp leg, and when we got to the southern elevation I told him that tree over there is the finish line, that we'd play around a little, not exactly run like kids, just get him moving around a bit, try to warm up his rheumatic leg—come on, tag me, I said, and he came at me, dragging that leg, I ran backward, said come on, faster, I'm close to the line, he was gasping, exhausted from dragging his leg in my direction, drooling from pure excitement—Otávio, time had passed by him, too, plopped down, steadied one of his hands against a stone: Otávio's tired, I said, he wants to go home, doesn't he?

When we got back, I asked Kurt to lend me the car for the first time. I need to go back to Porto Alegre, I said. You don't have a driver's license, he replied. I told him not to worry. Otávio was sitting on the porch steps, bending over to look at an anthill.

I found a parking space on Riachuelo, and

went walking down Borges. There, from Largo de Prefeitura all the way to Rua da Praia, a dense crowd was shouting. A windy night, a pamphlet blew between my legs. On the corner of Salgado Filho I asked a creole woman what was going on. She told me it was a rally for Lula, but he hadn't arrived yet. A man was giving a speech on the platform, flags, everyone fired up. It was December, and there was an even fuller moon than the night before. Ah, next Sunday was the presidential election, the runoff, I mumbled to myself, so the creole woman couldn't hear.

What time is Lula supposed to arrive? I asked the creole woman, who I now saw was rather sexy, well put together, and she said she didn't know, she'd been there since five and the crowd just kept growing—she was talking and I couldn't respond with more than an ah…the thing was that I'd never banged a creole and I thought the time had come. I noticed it was already a different voice speaking from the platform, but I couldn't hear anything the guy was saying because the crowd was shouting campaign slogans, a group was passing by singing a

Carnival marching tune with the lyrics all changed to other words that I couldn't understand amid the ruckus, and the creole woman was right there in front of me, her plump mouth wouldn't stop moving—commenting on the rally I guess—wearing a low-cut blouse so I could almost see her entire breasts, heaving, sweaty, and excited to tell me everything about the rally.

It's so damn hot, I said, why don't we go have a beer while we wait for Lula?

We went down Rua da Praia, the sounds of a drum circle on the corner of Uruguai mixing with the sound of beer cans rolling along the ground, kicked along consciously or not. Later, a man brandishing a Bible with a black cover fumed to anyone who'd listen that this cannot be, this cannot be. A street kid was fooling around, mimicking the man, pretending to stab him with something when his back was turned, and the crowd laughed, laughed at the kid, only I couldn't laugh, because the boy was the spitting image of me as a child, it was just a question of glancing at the portrait I carried in my wallet, from when I was eight, nine years old max, with a Grêmio club T-shirt, the one taken by my father in Parque da Redenção: look at this, I showed the photo to the creole woman—what's your name again? I remembered to ask, Naíra, she replied, Naíra, I repeated, look, this kid in the photo is me, and I ask you, the boy who was just here trying to fuck with the guy with the Bible in his hand, that boy has the same face as mine in this photo, right? Who is he? Naíra asks. I'm going to go find out, I reply. Naíra says she never saw a resemblance like that, even in twins, so then I go brandishing the photo until I find the boy, still entertaining himself with the man with the Bible in his hand, and when the boy sees me he takes off running, clearly afraid that I'm a cop, and the man with the Bible in his hand comes over and puts his face into mine and in his thick rasp says, if we're going crazy it's because God is making us crazy, if we return to sanity it's for the rest of you, Corinthians—and then he pointed to my chest, saying that those were the words of Saint Paul, the words of Saint Paul, I repeated, and suddenly he reminded me of a priest from back at the church in Glória who used to talk to me when I

was more or less the age of the boy in the photo—
he told me about the letters of Saint Paul to the
Corinthans, Corinthians, Corinthonians, whatever,
that priest would say: the purest poetry you could
ever want to read, when you're bigger you'll see...
and I turned to Naíra, half-stunned, and embraced
her madly, and thus entwined we kept on walking.

And we sat on a bench in the Praça da
Alfândega, where a guy with a styrofoam cooler was
selling cans of beer. Naíra and I toasted by tapping
our cans together—this was how I was trying to
forget the existence of a boy with my face running
around here, a boy that, if he wanted, could someday
pass for me—and I slipped my hand down Naíra's
blouse, her warm tit was tender and swollen, and
after letting out a long deep sigh she told me, look,
here comes the boy, and sure enough there he was,
heading for the docks, and here he came—amaz-
ing!—holding hands with the man with the Bible in
his hand, as though they were heading home after a
long day's work—there the two of them went, and
I shrugged, whatever, deciding to let it go. I noticed
a few tramps around our bench lustily ogling as I

felt up Naíra. Well, they'll be treated to a lot more than that tonight, and, for the first time, I kissed the plump mouth of a black woman, and she was one of those women who dominate a man's mouth with her ferocious tongue, her tongue struggled for primacy inside my mouth, like she was trying to dig out my cavities—I pushed her away, took a breath, and said c'mon, let's go somewhere we can be alone, c'mon, and we got up, still clinging to each other, and clinging to each other took long steps down Rua da Praia. Borges was roaring from the rally, a voice from up on the platform said that Lula's plane had just landed at Salgado Filho airport, popcorn was bursting, and Naíra and I kept on clinging to each other as we made our way to the car I'd left parked on Riachuelo.

When I put my hands on the wheel Naíra told me she had her own place. I asked where. She said it was on Marcílio Dias, near Érico Veríssimo.

We'd already turned down Marcílio and were passing by a row of low houses when Naíra said: it's one of these, park right here, but she said it at the last second and I only managed to stop two or three

houses later, in front of a door with a plaque adver-
tising umbanda supplies. Naíra put a hand on my
arm and asked me to go a little further, closer to the
corner. I told her I was confused, had we passed her
house or not? Go a little further, she insisted. Here,
she said, in front of what looked like an abandoned
lot hemmed in by old hedges. Come, she murmured
with her eyes darting around, and she started pulling me, ducking through a hole in the hedge—the
other side, sure enough, was an abandoned lot.

By this point Naíra was lighting a joint, she
offered it to me—I thought it was a great idea to
have a little toke, and I took three, four deep hits,
feeling great, but I hadn't come all this way just to
get stoned—I was crazy for something I'd always
been dying to see: a white cock going into a black
woman's pussy. I imagined that inside her I'd find a
tone to shock a whitey like me, and the very bright
moonlight would make clear every doubt and detail,
and I confirmed once more that the moon was really
full, resplendent even, and I put Naíra up against the
remains of a wall that still endured in the middle
of the lot, lifted her skirt, opened my pants—cum

outside, Naíra said—and I plunged all the way into her wetness and she moaned, oh wow.

The moon wasn't as friendly as I'd hoped—I could barely see any parts of the creole woman who was now quivering and sliding down the wall until she fell on the dirt. And her skirt, now still, had flapped around the whole time, and my shirt was so long I'd had to keep pushing it out of the way with my hand—all that cloth didn't let me see things very well. But, with respect to Naíra's drowning wetness: it felt like she was pissing on my hard-on the whole time.

Naíra stayed sitting in the dirt, I got down to see where she was, groping around—it was the wet dirt she seemed to like. You like it? I murmured. Like what? she asked. Sitting here, I replied.

I might as well repeat that the moon was full, and can add that it was orange, and also add, or repeat, I don't remember, that with the breeze you couldn't exactly call it a hot night, only hot enough to wet through your shirt in the middle of the crowd at the rally, but Naíra…let's go back. Naíra was sitting at my feet, saying something, telling me she lost her virginity when she was thirteen to a cracker German from São Sebastião do Caí: just think, to be born as black as I am and raised in the middle of those crazy blondes in Caí, well that's how it was, my father worked at the slaughterhouse, when I was a girl I killed time on Saturday afternoons by going to see the cattle lined up, waiting their turn, and when they got close they'd start to moo desperately, that was my hobby, cattle moaning so loud you could hear them halfway around the world, to this day I can't forget the sound of it, I'd crouch down by the fence for the whole afternoon looking at them, they wouldn't let you get very close, they wouldn't let anybody who didn't work there jump the fence, Naíra, I said, Naíra, should we go? She said my fly was still open, which it was—I slipped my hand through my fly, gave a tug on my shirt so it wouldn't stay sticking out of my pants, even down there my shirt was covered in cum, the moon full, the wind somewhat refreshing, pulling Naíra's hand so she'd come with me, Naíra's skirt all dirty, the two of us going through the hole in the hedge, looking around to make sure nobody saw, a whistling man coming down the street went by without looking and stopped on the corner without hesitation, as though that were his place, Naíra taking off her high heels, walking away barefoot without even saying goodbye, me seated in the car, picking out a tape from the glove box, a trusty Bach of Kurt's, there wasn't anything else, I put on the Bach, hit the gas, the moon full, December, the starry sky and everything else…

What was he doing there, in the kitchen, with his arms crossed over the table, the low lamp brightening his rope-veined hands? What was he doing there, at that time of night, when I got back to the manor? What was he, Kurt, doing there like I'd never seen him before, it looked like he'd shrunk, yes, he who had been so imposing before was now a man diminished in stature, sitting there in the kitchen under the low lamp—ah, there was a glass, and beside it a bottle of a cachaça called Isaura, beside that a Coke, empty. Long live the samba-in-Berlin, I growled, pulling out the paper napkin with the poem that I'd kept in my pocket ever since we got on the plane in Galeão—a name for it still hadn't come to me, I wondered if "Quiet Creature on the Corner" wasn't the title the poem was asking for—Kurt followed me with his eyes, raised the glass like he was toasting me, ah, so he was drunk, I didn't know how drunk, only the silence of the glass in his hand. I, in the doorway of the kitchen, thinking it was the first time I'd seen Kurt drunk, I stood in the kitchen doorway wondering if I really wanted to go in and continue with the farce that was unfolding, Kurt tremblingly raising the glass, toasting me, I couldn't stand him drunk, not Kurt, I could tell the night was hanging by a thread, I could tell what I was observing was an invitation: an old man widowed just hours prior beckoning me into the tavern to keep him company, to drink, drink until dawn with an unhappy man, that was the idea—but if someday a miracle were to burst over me, that miracle would come from him: that was what I needed to believe in, a chance I couldn't throw away because it would never be repeated, but I wondered, I wondered what this man could have besides the skeleton of a cow, a peeling mansion, a sad piece of land, whatever business Gerda had in Germany…

I took a few steps, tried to say gently: let's go to Germany, let's not let Gerda's death keep us from going.

Kurt lowered the glass, said his plans were kaput, his body diseased—for years now—and from now on he didn't think he'd be in any condition to travel, for a while now he hadn't been able to urinate right, he showed me his swollen feet, darkly swollen, he was getting headaches that drove him near to the point of despair, said it was an abscess, definitely, but keep it a secret because I hate doctors, no doctor is going to touch me, they see everything here inside, and inside here there's nothing worth seeing, what's interesting lives out in the light of day, I'll unbutton my shirt and show you the blotch on my chest, every day it spreads, for a long time I didn't let Gerda see my bare chest, she didn't know about the blotch, she always believed I was a strong man, but I'm not going to die, not now.

I sat down at the other end of the table and thought, I don't want this: What good did it do me to have him bail me out of jail just to get caught up in illness and old age? First Gerda, then Otávio, and tonight I get home and find him drunk and besides that all rotten, telling me he's not going to die. What do I get out of this?

Or, if I wasn't going to get anything from it, why was he telling me all this? Wouldn't I be better off among the prisoners, who lacked any appetite for reward? Or in that clinic where nobody demanded my company, where books of poems appeared without me asking for them, where I couldn't expect any more than that, maybe I'd be better off there?

But then came this man who brought me here to lick his wounds.

I stuck my tongue out of my mouth, in the direction of my chin—for the first time in my life I thought that I had my own heart, which beat so many times per minute—I thought about touching the vein in my wrist, counting, I thought about the occult organization of those to whom obedience is owed, I thought that being here before this old man was to obey this same organization—my tongue was now prowling up above my mouth, frightened by the prickle of the mustache that had begun to form, my tongue was passing all around my mouth. Kurt had a dim stare, and I was sure that in that moment he couldn't distinguish me from the sur-roundings, but a breath would bring the exact word to my lips, capable of reactivating the senses of the man in front of me, the exact word flowering on my lips would bring him back to my image, my compa-ny, and I'd try to swallow everything again, as if this were all a game of patience:

"Kurt!" I called out.

"Huh?" he tried to straighten up, "you're back?"

"Listen to the hoot of that owl," I said devilishly.

"The owl's hoot, I'd like to hear the owl's hoot," he said, looking around, searching.

I got up, opened a can of sardines. I went back to sit in front of Kurt. I emptied the can of every last morsel and wiped it clean with a hunk of bread.

The dogs were barking in the distance—I had no interest in knowing where those beasts were imprisoned.

He told me he'd heard a voice calling for Amália. He said: God knows who'd be calling her, maybe some stranger who's trying to use her to take charge around here, invading little by little until not a trace of me is left.

"Plot by plot," I remarked, without a clear idea of what the words meant.

"Plot by plot," he emphasized.

Kurt seemed blind. He was staring at the refrigerator, but beneath his gaze the refrigerator appeared as a shape without any likeness, strange even to itself, on the verge of dissolving.

I got up, took a few steps toward Kurt: if as long as all this lasted I stayed close, not letting anything escape me, yes, I wouldn't regret it later—it was in this difficult thing that I needed to believe.

Otávio appeared at the kitchen door. There was silence. Only Otávio's huffy breathing. He was wearing pajamas that were all frayed at the edges, suspiciously stained, a beret on his head, I could tell now it was a uniform beret, a Brazilian Expeditionary Force beret.

Kurt was still staring at the refrigerator—it was possible that he'd found a way to fill the dead hours before dawn.

Otávio, in his dirty pajamas and expeditionary beret, and right behind him just then, right on his tail, appeared Amália with half-indecisive steps,

JOÃO GILBERTO NOLL

Amália avoiding my eyes, as though she were trying to convey her shame—following Otávio out
from some hiding place I might not know about, I
thought to myself. Otávio looked at me and said:

"I put on my BEF beret and came to get a drink
of water."

"You sleep in that beret?" I asked.

"No," he was shaking like he wanted to laugh at
my question, but was obviously too weak.

"No?" I insisted.

"It's just a little obsession," he said softly, "I
bring the beret to bed with me. Ever since I got
back from Italy, I go to sleep with the feeling that
during the night the enemy will come and I need to
be prepared."

I noticed the beret was really worn out, mis-
shapen, saturated by the kind of care that children
show the ragged things they won't get rid of.

Amália came out from behind him, filled a glass
of cold water, and took it to Otávio, who was still
standing in the same place, not having budged from
the threshold.

Maybe it was visible, the sacrifice that was being

imposed on me by who knows whose designs—accepting the nauseating contact with these creatures until I was completely consumed—and so yes, instead of being a man ready to act.

While Otávio was gulping down the water, Amália stared at me. She had a thread of blood along her lower lip. I saw Kurt staring at her, caught off guard. Otávio handed the glass back to her and also stared at her, until she asked if he wanted more.

"No," Otávio mumbled, now staring at me.

No, I repeated without knowing why. Sometimes a word slips out of me like that, before I have time to formalize an intention in my head. Sometimes on such occasions it comes to me with relief, as though I've felt myself distilling something that only once finished and outside me, I'll be able to know.

Otávio doesn't want any more, I concluded with an indecisive tone.

"No," Otávio reaffirmed.

"No," said Kurt, returning his gaze to the refrigerator.

I yawned, looking at the white of the refrigerator.

Then I belched a little from the sardines.

I said goodnight and withdrew.

As I made my way out I paid attention to the abnormal silence in the kitchen. I wanted to go back and see what was happening there inside the inertia the whole atmosphere seemed to have fallen into, but no, tomorrow I'd finish out another whole day with them, and if the three were to drown in that silence, then tomorrow I'd declare my conspiracy finished, finally, hallelujah.

I closed the door to my room and I wasn't sad. You might say that the two old men and I don't know what else left me limp with sadness, but it was nothing like that: when I took off my clothes I caught a whiff of Naíra's scandalous scent on my body, it was nice to slip my hand across myself and sniff it, as though that sultry odor were coming from my own skin.

No, I wasn't sad, and when I turned off the light something came over me: I fell to the floor on all fours and began to feel a strange momentum first to crawl, then drag, myself, in silence, as though the floor were a battlefield swamp, guessing where the next bomb would go off as they flashed closer and closer.

In the morning, when I awoke, I would remember: I had submitted to this like a man, and
I was prepared to master these events, which had
confused me before.

I could sense that someone had opened the
door to my room, there was no noise, only the light
from the hall washing over me a little—I considered
sitting up and turning my head to look at whoever
was watching me. But it wasn't worth it: that presence was incapable of threatening my submerged
state, bordering on sleep. I blacked out completely.

I awoke on the hard floor, ran a hand through
my sweat, looked at the closed door, suddenly remembered—but there was no sign of the presence
that had come and gone.

I got up, turned on the lights, and sat on the bed.
I looked at my legs, which appeared to be reasonably
muscular. I was a man, not the spring chicken that
had come here with Kurt. I was a man and I was not
in love. Naíra's scent was still clinging to my body,
I was indecisive about which tack to take while the
old German still breathed, that protector of a whole
man like me, with well-formed muscles—how I

acquired them I honestly didn't know—I knew now that I'd been a man a long time, without adequate conditions for taking a position as long as Kurt existed, but I'd be able to start doing things, making certain preparations, though I still couldn't say what they'd be—I stared at the muscles in my leg, I was a man and I was not in love.

I wore Naíra's scent, and the best I could do was go back to sleep, this time on the soft mattress, hugging one of the pillows, the kind of sleep that maybe wouldn't come from just lying in bed—maybe I'd rather just roll around and excite myself with Naíra's fading scent, maybe just keep repeating that I was a man, and that the next day I'd see to things.

I'd barely hit the mattress when I heard a sob, which seemed at first like it was coming from inside the pillow—a rough crying, not that of a woman—when I opened the door to Kurt's room, he was in bed all curled up, crying: I need to man up, I need to man up, was what my head then began to hammer, but I needed to think of something else, urgently—get close to Kurt's body, not rest until I'd made a clear gesture to this man whom I'd known to be so proud and who was now crying this rough sob.

He had turned into a weak subject, old from head to toe, and now that the moment of my entrance had arrived, I didn't know whether to divert or interrupt what was waiting there for me to find out.

I sat on the bed. I thought about what I should do, if anything, or if all this wasn't much more than a comedy I'd better avoid. The sobbing continued, without pause, and I said to myself: maybe I'll lie down, stay lying here beside him and wait, because he'll get tired of crying, oh yes, crying is tiresome. Soon after, he slowly calmed: I was lying beside him and he was calming down—I wonder if I'm hearing right, as Kurt began to breathe deeply like a cat demonstrating satisfaction with something nearby—Kurt purring at my side, until he ended up exposing something unappealing to me, that old purrer, lying at my side uncurling, turning to me, looking at me with his eyes open only to the inside, as though he didn't think there was anything to look at in my place, as though my body were nothing more than a continuation of the bed.

Suddenly Kurt whispered, Gerda. I pulled the

cord on the lamp—I didn't want to look at him, I wanted only to calm a vague sense of urgency inside, and tried to reflect: may he at least still have the time necessary for me to prepare a satisfactory life.

Because I deserved at least that, a satisfactory life—in old age I'd sit and watch the misty fields of my patch of earth, throwing feed to the birds nearby, a blanket across my knees—flannel like the one I was now holding in Kurt's bed.

Kurt rolled onto my arm, and I thought about how useless I was with my arm already falling asleep beneath Kurt's body, and he rolled up onto my chest, and his weight at first almost suffocated me, but I breathed deeply, settled myself, opened my arms, I opened my clenched hands too, and then I saw Kurt's face from very, very close, almost up against mine, and Kurt's face had begun to cry again, this time silently, a whorl of wrinkles, a mute but enormous wail, huge, and I wouldn't know how, even with him so old and weak, there was anything I could do to evaporate that elephantine wailing that flattened me against the mattress—where were my reasonable muscles?—I thought I'd been a man for a

while, but now I'd fallen into the net, through a trap-
door, this weight didn't even allow me the possibility
of saying anything but a faint it's okay, it's okay, and
Kurt began heaving, bringing up from within him
something I couldn't contain, his samba-in-Berlin
breath right in my mouth, and I kept repeating it's
okay, it's okay, I couldn't even see how atrociously
ridiculous it was or anything: only a daze that left
me repeating it's okay, it's okay.

Yes, at that moment I could say I was sad.
Atop my body, Kurt was now just dead weight,
pure survival, with his head buried in my shoulder,
folded into the space where it met my neck. I was
sad for having been a man who couldn't oppose
this advance, a full-grown man, with normal muscles, unable to react to that old mass, who couldn't
guarantee him anything but a roof, pocket money,
tedious company, who guaranteed him nothing
more than that.

I took pains to disentangle myself from the de-
fenseless weight, the old man's life was regressing
to the wet farts he was letting out, continuously,
miasmas of samba-in-Berlin—I slowly opened the

blinds, noticed day was about to break through, not a moment too soon, not a single bird was singing, not even the usual rooster, still only the crickets—what suggested day was about to break was an almost invisible vibration behind the hillside, which is to say that it was as cold as that time of day required, and I was, by instinct, unsurprised when I saw a bonfire near the lake, only later did I say to myself: Why is Amália setting another fire, throwing all those things in it to burn?

I got dressed and went to the fire, didn't find Amália: it looked like a party had just ended, at the base of the fire things were already unrecognizable, twisted, various flames around them, but one thing I recognized, the BEF beret—I first saw a tongue of flame licking the band, then the emblem was twisted upward by the tallest flame, Otávio's beret had been thrown on the fire last, only now was it beginning to be destroyed—I took a rod, stirred the fire, and pushed what remained intact of the beret into the middle of the bonfire—I wondered what it was doing there, if Otávio knew about it, if for some incomprehensible reason it had been his idea, if he had come with Amália to admire the objects being consumed and had decided to toss in his expeditionary beret, or if not, if Amália had stolen the beret from him to destroy it in the dead of night, the night which was at that moment ending: there behind the hill a band of blue, above that violet, I could say for the last time before the daytime definitively arrived that there were stars in the sky, the moon full, or maybe say that I was a man and I wasn't in love, for the tenth, eleventh time, but I preferred to remain silent, gaze at the lake filling with light, the dark and muddy lake that, in the timid start to morning, seemed to mirror another landscape, some sort of chalky plane, maybe from the thin mist, but a color so light that I began to doubt.

I went in. When my feet felt the cold, freezing water, the old rooster crowed. Then the murmur of birds, the crickets' slow paralysis—no, it isn't important, because this is what I want to say: the water was freezing cold and I kept going deeper.

Then I swam breaststroke, sliding, sometimes floating on my back and confirming that the day had already overtaken the entire sky, a clear

December day—I flipped over to try the butterfly, and as I turned I noticed that Kurt was on the shore watching me.

Over his pajamas he wore a black overcoat, and in his hand, his arm outstretched, he was offering me some clothes I didn't recognize as mine: I figured they must have been some of his.

I looked down, I was where I could no longer stand, I moved my legs like I was riding a bicycle, sometimes sinking a little toward the bottom, just until my head went under, then I'd return to the surface and see Kurt smiling at me in a way I'd never seen before, like someone who smiles because they feel themselves to be small before a situation—he was offering me clothes from the tip of his outstretched hand, and I kept returning to the depths, counting to find out how long my breath would last beneath the lake, on the next submersion staying longer, then opening my mouth to pull all the air into my lungs, submerging my head once more, and then emerging again, my eyes above water, Kurt smiling, not saying anything, he was showing me the clothes I should trade for these soaking wet ones, what he was offering me was a striped shirt and dark pants, there, on the shore of the lake, and I put my head underwater again, I thought about counting once more how many seconds I could withstand, but I said, no, I'll go over there, I'll take those clothes, I won't even button the shirt, it will be hot today, then I'll see about what to do—and then I came to the surface, took two or three strokes, then I started walking on the gelatinous lake bed, suddenly I was stepping on the pebbles of the shore—I needed to accept those clothes Kurt was offering in his trembling hand, and when I got close something came over me like a poison, and I yelled, I ripped the wet shirt from my body with one movement, I tore it, the buttons flying, in a fit I stripped off my pants and underwear, furiously kicking my leg to untangle myself from my pants, and now I'd dress in the dry clothes Kurt was handing me, and then I'd go to bed, calm myself, sleep, and maybe even dream.

JOÃO GILBERTO NOLL is the author of nearly 20 books. His work has appeared in Brazil's leading periodicals, and he has been a guest of the Rockefeller Foundation, King's College London, and the University of California at Berkeley, as well as a Guggenheim Fellow. A five-time recipient of the Prêmio Jabuti, he lives in Porto Alegre, Brazil.

ADAM MORRIS has a PhD in Latin American literature from Stanford University and was the recipient of the 2012 Susan Sontag Foundation Prize in literary translation. He is the translator of Hilda Hilst's *With My Dog-Eyes* (Melville House Books, 2014). His writing and translations have been published widely, including in *BOMB* magazine, the *Los Angeles Review of Books*, and many others. He lives in San Francisco.